Emmy
the Exaggerating
Elephant

Fenton
the Fearful Frog

Gertie
the Grungy Goat

He...
the Happy
Hamster

Ivy
the Impatient
Iguana

Ollie
the Obedient
Ostrich

Perry
the Polite
Porcupine

Queenie
the Quiet Quail

Rupert
the Resourceful
Rhinoceros

Wendy
the Wise
Woodchuck

Xavier
the X-ploring
Xenops

Yori
the Yucky Yak

Ziggy
the Zippy Zebra

NOTE TO PARENTS

Connie the Cuddly Cat is feeling lonely and wants to play with someone. But all of her AlphaPet friends are too busy. Even though the AlphaPets don't mean to hurt Connie's feelings, their actions lead Connie to think that they don't care about her. Feeling rejected and unloved, Connie decides to run away. Once they realize how upset she is, Connie's friends search for her to show her how much they truly do care about her. But will they find her in time?

As you read **Connie, Come Home** and discuss the pictures with your child, use the story to introduce the letter **Cc**. When the letter **Cc** begins a word within the text, the **Cc** is highlighted to emphasize the letter and to help your child recognize it. As you read the story again, ask your child to listen for the **Cc** words, and help your child to find the objects whose names begin with **Cc.**

In addition to enjoying this story and learning about the letter **Cc,** your child will begin to understand that friends should take special care to consider each other's feelings and needs. One friend's actions—intentional or not—can affect how another friend feels and reacts. Your child will also learn that when one friend hurts another friend, it is important to apologize and to try to be more sensitive the next time. The story can also lead to a discussion about how to accept an apology.

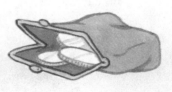

The AlphaPet™ characters were conceived and created by Ruth Lerner Perle.
Characters interpreted and designed by Deborah Colvin Borgo.
Cover design by Antler & Baldwin Design Group.
Book design and production by Nancy Norton.
Logo design by Deborah Colvin Borgo and Nancy Norton.

ISBN: 0-7172-8759-9

Connie, Come Home

RUTH LERNER PERLE

Illustrated by Deborah Colvin Borgo

 Grolier Books
Danbury, Connecticut

One day, **C**onnie the **C**uddly **C**at was feeling bored and lonely.

She didn't want to read.

She didn't want to watch TV.

She didn't want a **c**up of **c**ocoa.

She didn't even want the piece of **c**ake she'd **c**ut.

Connie wanted to play with a friend.

As she looked out the window. **C**onnie saw Wendy
the Wise Woodchuck hurrying by her house.

"Wendy!" **C**onnie **c**alled. "Will you **c**ome and play
with me?"

"I **c**an't right now," Wendy said. "I'm late for my **c**larinet lesson. Why don't you play with Gertie the Grungy Goat?"

"Good idea," thought **C**onnie. So she put on her
coat and **c**ap and walked over to Gertie's house.

Since Gertie's door was broken, **C**onnie knocked
on the house.
"**C**ome in!" Gertie **c**alled.

Connie took one step inside. But she **c**ouldn't take another.

Her shoe was stuck in a glob of gooey gum. *Yuck!*
Connie pulled and pulled. At last, she pulled her foot free.

Gertie was talking on the telephone.

"Excuse me, Gertie," Connie whispered. "Will you play with me?"

"I'm busy just now," said Gertie. "Maybe later."

"All right," Connie said sadly. And she left Gertie's house.

Connie went to the park.

There, she found Rupert the Resourceful Rhinoceros. He was skipping from tree to tree.

"Oh, Rupert!" Connie called. "May I skip with you?"

"I'm not skipping! I'm collecting chestnuts," said Rupert.

As he ran to show the bag of **c**hestnuts to **C**onnie, he tripped and fell.

Kerplunk!

The bag broke and all the **c**hestnuts **c**ame rolling out. "Oh no!" Rupert groaned. "Now I have to get another bag." And off he ran.

Poor **C**onnie was alone once again.

Connie visited some of her other friends. But they were busy, too.

Lizzy the Lazy Lamb was taking a nap.

Albert the Absent-minded Alligator was looking for his glasses.

Perry the Polite Porcupine was writing thank-you notes.

And Yori the Yucky Yak was taking his spiders for a walk.

So **C**onnie headed for the market. There she met Delilah the Demanding Duck.

"Hello, Delilah. Want to play?" **C**onnie asked.

"Play? Play? I don't want to play. I want **c**aramel **c**andy and **c**oconut **c**ookies!" Delilah hurried away, leaving **C**onnie alone—again.

Connie slowly walked home.

When **C**onnie reached her house, she started
to **c**ry.

"Nobody loves me. Nobody **c**ares," she sobbed.
"I'm leaving AlphaPet **C**orners. I'll go live with
Cousin **C**ora."

So **C**onnie packed her things. Then she wrote a
good-bye note and left it on the table.

She grabbed her suitcase, her doll, and an
umbrella. And off she went to the bus station.

Before long

Wendy's **c**larinet lesson was over.

Gertie was off the phone.

Rupert's **c**hestnuts were all **c**ollected.

And Delilah was done shopping.

Now *all* the AlphaPets had some free time and they missed their friend **C**onnie. So, one by one, they went over to **C**onnie's house.

But **C**onnie wasn't home. "Where **c**ould she be?" the AlphaPets wondered. Then they found her note and they were sad.

"Let's try to find **C**onnie and bring her back," said Rupert.

"Oh yes! We must find her!" Delilah demanded.

"Good idea," added Yori.

"If **C**onnie is going to her **c**ousin **C**ora's house, she'll be taking the bus. Maybe she's still at the station!" Wendy said.

Everybody hurried to the bus station. And sure enough, there was **C**onnie!

"Oh, **C**onnie, please don't go," **c**ried the AlphaPets.

"But I thought you didn't **c**are about me," **C**onnie said.

"Of **c**ourse we **c**are about you," they replied. "We're sorry we were so busy earlier today."

BUS STOP

Just then, a big green bus pulled up and
the doors opened. "All aboard!" called
the driver.

Connie picked up her suitcase.

"Please stay," everyone called. "You're
our friend and we love you!"

Slowly, Connie climbed up the bus steps.

"You'd better leave without me," **C**onnie said to the driver. "I'm staying with my friends."

"Whoopee!!" everyone **c**heered. And they all went home together.

Here are the words I love most. They all start with the **c**uddly letter **Cc,** just like me!

cup

coat

carrot

car

calendar

cookies

comb

corn

can

cake

Look back at pictures and words in this book.
See if you **c**an find the pictures or words above,
as well as others that begin with the letter **Cc.**

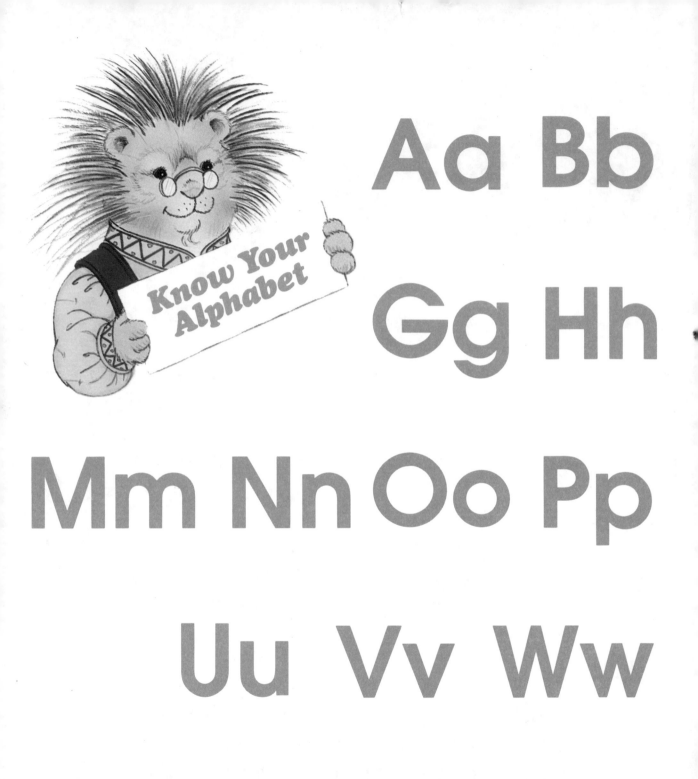

Aa Bb

Gg Hh

Mm Nn Oo Pp

Uu Vv Ww